Pip Pip Pip

Written by Zoë Clarke

Illustrated by Mónica Armiño

Collins

T0337122

A sad man sits.

sip

sip

sip

3

It is a pip.

pip

pip

pip

Tap it in.

tip

tap

tip

tap

7

Pat it in.

pit

pat

pit

pat

9

Sit in a dip.

A man did it.

After reading

Letters and Sounds: Phase 2

Word count: 42

Focus phonemes: /s/ /a/ /t/ /p/ /i/ /n/ /m/ /d/

Common exception word: is

Curriculum links: Understanding the World: People and Communities; The World

Early learning goals: Listening and attention: listen to stories, accurately anticipating key events and respond to what is heard with relevant comments, questions or actions; Understanding: answer 'how' and 'why' questions about experiences and in response to stories or events; Reading: children use phonic knowledge to decode regular words and read them aloud accurately; they also read some common irregular words; they demonstrate understanding when talking with others about what they have read.

Developing fluency

- Go back and read the chant to your child, using lots of expression.
- Make sure that your child follows as you read.
- Pause so they can join in and read with you.
- Say the whole chant together. You can make up some actions to go with the words.

A sad man sits.	Tap it in.	Sit in a dip.
sip sip sip	tip tap tip tap	nip nip nip
It is a pip.	Pat it in.	A man did it.
pip pip pip	pit pat pit pat	tip tip tip

Phonic practice

- Point to the word **sip** on page 3. Model sounding it out 's-i-p' and blending the sounds together **sip**. Ask your child to do the same.
- Can they look in the story and find any words that rhyme with **sip**? (e.g. *pip, tip, dip, nip*)
- Now look at the I spy sounds pages (14–15) together. Which words can your child find in the picture with the /i/ or /m/ sounds in them? (e.g. *moon, quill, pins, nib*)